The Turtle and the Moon

by Charles Turner

illustrated by Melissa Bay Mathis

A Puffin Unicorn

DUTTON CHILDREN'S BOOKS NEW YORK

For Jonathan, Curt, and Kathryn
C. T.

For my brother John, whose presence in my life
makes all the difference
M. B. M.

PUFFIN UNICORN BOOKS

Published by the Penguin Group
Penguin Books USA Inc., 375 Hudson Street, New York, New York 10014, U.S.A.
Penguin Books Ltd, 27 Wrights Lane, London W8 5TZ, England
Penguin Books Australia Ltd, Ringwood, Victoria, Australia
Penguin Books Canada Ltd, 10 Alcorn Avenue, Toronto, Ontario, Canada M4V 3B2
Penguin Books (N.Z.) Ltd, 182-190 Wairau Road, Auckland 10, New Zealand
Penguin Books Ltd, Registered Offices: Harmondsworth, Middlesex, England

Library of Congress number 90-43841   ISBN 0-14-055812-8
Published in the United States by Dutton Children's Books, a division of Penguin Books USA Inc.
Designer: Riki Levinson   Printed in Hong Kong by South China Printing Co.
First Puffin Unicorn Edition 1996
3 5 7 9 10 8 6 4

THE TURTLE AND THE MOON is also available
in hardcover from Dutton Children's Books.

The turtle lived alone
in the tall grass beside the lake.

Every day he went for a walk
and then he took a nap,

and then he dived into the water
and went for a swim.

Then he took a sunbath

and went for another swim.

Sometimes the turtle got lonely
because there was nobody to play with.

At the end of the day,
even before the sun went down,
the turtle would draw himself into his shell
and go to sleep.

But one restless night he woke up
and poked his head out
and saw something so big
and so round and so strange
that he snapped at it.

The moon—for that was what it was—slid behind a cloud.
"I'm sorry I frightened you," the turtle said.
"Come out and I promise not to snap at you again."
But the moon did not come out.
"Come out and let's go for a swim," the turtle said.
But the moon did not come out

"I bet you *can't* swim," the turtle scoffed.
 And then the moon peeped out.
"I'll race you," the turtle challenged,
 and he turned and lumbered toward the lake.

But when he poked his nose through the tall grass,
the turtle was surprised.
The moon was already in the water, waiting for him.

The turtle threw himself into the shining lake
—plop!—

and suddenly the moon was splashing around,
playing hide-and-seek and tag,
diving down here,
bobbing up there,
shimmering in every direction.

"Show-off," the turtle said,
  and he began to show off too,
  swimming in circles,
  ducking his head,
  kicking up his heels.

When the sun edged the horizon,
the turtle and the moon were very tired and very sleepy.
The turtle drew himself into his shell and slept.
The fading moon drifted to the other side of the lake,
to the other side of the world. . . .

Not a trace of it was left when the turtle woke up.
The turtle went for a walk as usual,
and then he took a nap as usual,

and then he dived into the water and went for a swim
and took a sunbath and went for another swim,
as usual.

But that evening the turtle did *not* go to bed
before dark, as usual.
That evening, he waited for the sun to go down,
for night to fall,

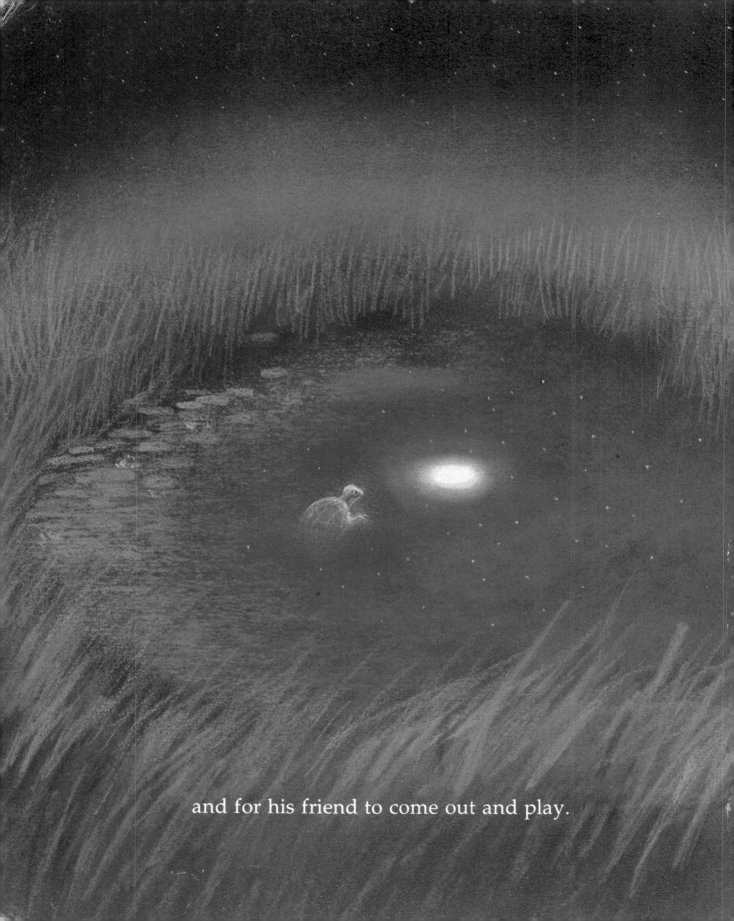

and for his friend to come out and play.